orca
limelights

Raw Talent

Jocelyn Shipley

ORCA BOOK PUBLISHERS

Library and Archives Canada Cataloguing in Publication

Shipley, Jocelyn, author
Raw talent / Jocelyn Shipley.
(Orca limelights)

Issued in print and electronic formats.
ISBN 978-1-4598-1834-7 (softcover).—ISBN 978-1-4598-1835-4 (PDF).—
ISBN 978-1-4598-1836-1 (EPUB)

I. Title. II. Series: Orca limelights
PS8587.H563R39 2018   jc813'.6   c2017-907696-5
c2017-907697-3

First published in the United States, 2018
Library of Congress Control Number: 2018933741

Summary: In this high-interest novel for teen readers, Paisley has to get over
her fear of performing in public if she ever wants to be a famous pop star.

*Orca Book Publishers is dedicated to preserving the environment and
has printed this book on Forest Stewardship Council® certified paper.*

Orca Book Publishers gratefully acknowledges the support
for its publishing programs provided by the following agencies:
the Government of Canada through the Canada Book Fund and the
Canada Council for the Arts, and the Province of British Columbia
through the BC Arts Council and the Book Publishing Tax Credit.

Edited by Tanya Trafford
Cover design by Rachel Page
Cover photography by Jonathan Caramanus/Stocksy.com

ORCA BOOK PUBLISHERS
orcabook.com

Printed and bound in Canada.

21 20 19 18 • 4 3 2 1

For Iris, Lauren, Lucas,
James, Eva and Seth

One

Help Save Sunflower Farm!
Can you sing? Dance? Play an instrument?
***FARMSHINE* needs you!**
Monday, 4 PM
Room 215

Looks like the posters Jasmeer made and that I helped put up all over the school really worked. The room is buzzing with excitement and energy. After our first planning meeting, word got around and now even more kids want to be involved. We're on a roll!

Vanessa, who's in twelfth grade and is head of the organizing committee, is sitting on the teacher's desk at the front of the room. "Okay, folks, let's get started!" she says, and we all go quiet.

"Thanks for coming today. My family is so, so, grateful that the students of Stonehill High are being so supportive."

Everybody claps and cheers.

Farmshine is a fundraiser for Sunflower Farm, which has been in Vanessa's family for generations. Ever since Vanessa's dad died in a snowmobile accident last spring, her mom has been struggling to manage the farm on her own. A land developer has offered to buy the land, but if we can raise enough money, Vanessa's mom can hire some workers to help and not have to sell the farm.

We've been talking in Socials about the importance of volunteering, so the fundraiser is a perfect idea. It will be a huge effort, but everybody loves Sunflower Farm. It's one of our local attractions with its fields of flowers, corn and pumpkins, its apple orchard and sugar bush. We all want to help. We'd do it even if we weren't getting credit for community service hours. Which we totally are, so bonus!

"First off, I've got some awesome news to share." Vanessa jumps off the desk. "Maxine Gaston has agreed to be our MC!"

The room explodes with gasps and shrieks. Maxine Gaston is a big deal. Everybody knows her from her role as Silver Spinner, the alien composer in the blockbuster movie *The Lost Song Galaxy*. She's also been in some popular TV series, and she often performs at the Stratford Festival near our town of Stonehill. Most of us have been on a school trip to Stratford and seen her in a play or musical.

"Settle down, settle down," Vanessa says. "I know it's exciting. But we've got a lot of other work to do. We're going to need tons of volunteers to run things, so tell your friends. Sound, lighting, backstage, front of house. And, of course, performers!"

Jasmeer pokes me in the ribs. "You're going to sign up, right?"

I glance over at Heath, Vanessa's younger brother. I've known him since fourth grade, and I've had a crush on him forever. I can't imagine how sad it must be for him and Vanessa to have lost their dad.

Heath doesn't look my way. No wonder. He's sitting beside Cadence Wang. They've been a thing since the summer.

Jasmeer pokes me again. "Right, Paisley?"

I really want to help Heath and Vanessa's family keep their farm. But I don't want to work backstage or sell tickets or be an usher. I want to perform.

Even though the idea totally terrifies me.

I don't sing in public. Not anymore.

My dream is to become a successful singer-songwriter. As a first step, I want to audition for our school musical next term. So I kind of have to get over my stage fright.

Farmshine could be my big chance.

"Hello?" Jasmeer says. "You didn't answer my question."

She knows how scared I am, although I haven't told her exactly why. I'm not sure she'd understand. She's into photography and can hide behind her camera. Up onstage, I'd be totally exposed. My stomach is already feeling woozy.

"Shh! I'm trying to hear what Vanessa's saying."

"Don't forget, everyone, that *Farmshine* is meant to showcase all the talents Stonehill has to offer. Some of you may not have heard that in addition to the performances onstage, there will also be a 'Farmer's Market' set up during inter-mission. We'll have flowers and produce from our farm, as well as crafts and baked goods for sale. So all you bakers and makers out there, be sure to sign up too."

More cheers and chatter. Vanessa passes around a clipboard with two sheets of paper. When it comes to Jasmeer, she puts her name on both the volunteer and the talent lists. She's volunteering to design the *Farmshine* program and set up the Facebook event page. She's also going to sell cards at the Farmer's Market made from photos she's taken of the farm.

"One more thing," Vanessa says. "We're still looking for a really big name to headline the show. Any suggestions?"

I've got a perfect one. Denzi, a pop star who actually grew up right here in Stonehill. She's even more famous than Maxine Gaston. And if Denzi came to *Farmshine*, I'd get to meet her! But the words don't come out. Not only am I scared to sing onstage, but I also don't even have the nerve to speak up here.

Heath does though. "How about Denzi?" he calls out.

Everybody starts chanting, "Denzi! Denzi! Denzi!"

"Whoa!" Vanessa yells. "Awesome idea, little brother! But it's *highly* unlikely she'd come. We have to be realistic."

Cadence stands and waits until everybody is looking at her. "The Sweetland Singers!" she says, flipping her long dark hair. "We're pretty famous too! And we're local."

Not to mention humble. I think I might barf.

"Great suggestion," Vanessa says. "Thanks, Cade."

"You're welcome. I'll ask our director at rehearsal tonight. Happy to help." Cadence smiles at Heath. "I'll probably have a solo. I'll dedicate it to Sunflower Farm and the memory of Heath and Vanessa's dad."

Definitely going to barf.

The Sweetland Singers *are* famous. They win all kinds of awards at music festivals. And after they won an international competition last summer, their name was added to the welcome sign on the road into town.

Okay, I will confess that I'm totally intimidated by the Sweetland Singers. I auditioned for them shortly after we moved here. Let's just say it didn't go well.

Jasmeer passes me the clipboard and pen. "Here you go."

I take it and read the names on the talent list. There are five pianists, three ballet dancers, a jazz troupe, an *a cappella* group, two rock bands and a ukulele player. So far.

I try to picture myself in the spotlight. Ready to sing.

But no. Just thinking about it makes me feel naked. And no way am I signing up if the Sweetland Singers are going to be the big-name act.

When Jasmeer isn't looking, I pass the clipboard on.

After the meeting Jasmeer and I head for our lockers. I'm just about to admit to her that I didn't sign up for anything when she says, "Oh my god! I'm so excited about *Farmshine*!"

"Yeah," I say. "Me too."

"It's going to be an amazing show. And I'm so proud of you for signing up! Way to go!"

"Um, about that..."

"Oh, don't stress over the stage-fright thing at all. I'm going to ask Maxine to coach you."

I stop and stare at her. "You mean Maxine Gaston, our MC?"

"Yes!"

"Seriously?" I say. "You really think she would?"

Maxine Gaston just happens to be staying at the B&B Jasmeer's parents run here in Stonehill while her house is being renovated. It's only a twenty-minute drive from here to Stratford, where she's currently performing in *The Merry Wives of Windsor*.

I met her at Thanksgiving dinner at Jasmeer's place. She's brilliant. I would love to have her help me overcome my stage fright. But oh wow, just the idea is petrifying.

"Maybe," Jasmeer says. "I mean, I'm sure she's super busy, but it can't hurt to ask."

Two

If Maxine Gaston will help me with my stage fright, I'll sign up to sing at *Farmshine* for sure. But that's a pretty safe promise. Because of course she'll say no. And then I'll just tell Jasmeer I never signed up and I'm never going to. End of story.

But that might mean the end of my singing career. Before it even gets started.

What to do? I wish I could decide.

When I get home from school, my parents are still at work, as usual. Which is fine by me, because it means I can sing with no one listening.

No reminders of what a disappointing daughter I am.

Here's the thing. My mom teaches music at a university and plays flute with a symphony.

When I was little, we took violin lessons together, but it was painful for both of us. After that I did learn some piano and how to read music. She wanted me to play classical composers and take the conservatory exams.

But all I've ever wanted to do is sing pop songs.

And my favorites are Denzi's songs.

Back in fourth grade, when we moved to Stonehill, I didn't want to leave my friends and the city. But then I found out that Denzi grew up here. She actually went to Stonehill High, same as me. Twenty years ago she was still just a small-town girl called Denise Zenkowski.

If she can make it big, so can I. Right?

Wrong. Because Denzi doesn't have stage fright. I've never seen her in person, but I've watched every video of her live concerts. She's such a confident performer. I am too, but only when I'm home alone, like now.

My mom would freak if she ever saw or heard me singing my heart out. My dad would be okay with it, but then he'd be in trouble with her. She's a pretty big music snob. If a piece wasn't written in Europe in, like, the eighteenth century or something, it doesn't rate.

Anyway, I practice and practice and practice, recording myself on my phone or tablet. Sometimes I do covers, sometimes my own songs. I've got notebooks full of lyrics and chords I've never shown anyone.

When I watch my videos, I truly believe I can be a star. But then I freeze. Somehow I just have to figure out how to make the move from singing in my bedroom to singing in public.

Jasmeer knows I like to sing, but I've never shown her any of my videos. Maybe I should. That might help me get used to other people seeing me sing. Give me the courage to post something on YouTube.

But I've only known her since high school started a couple of months ago. And I'm not sure it would make any difference at all. Someone watching me in a music video is not the same as someone watching me live onstage.

And now I'm upsetting myself thinking about all this. Okay, time to sing. That always makes me feel better.

I choose Denzi's greatest-hits album and sing along, holding my iPod up like a microphone. I know every word by heart. When "Somewhere the Music Shines Bright," the theme song from *The Lost Song Galaxy*, starts, I imagine Maxine Gaston introducing me onstage at *Farmshine.*

I hit the first notes in perfect pitch. I sing with passion to my adoring audience. Things are going great until I imagine my mom sitting in the front row. She looks furious. And right beside her is the director of the Sweetland Singers, horrified.

Suddenly I can't breathe. I can't remember the words. Shaking all over, I collapse on my bed.

Oh my god! What if I try to sing at *Farmshine* and that really happens?

My stage fright started with the Sweetland Singers. When we moved to Stonehill, my mom took me to see them at a summer concert in the park. They sang a variety of songs, folk, classical and world music, not pop. But they were excellent.

Afterward the director, Ms. Winton, announced auditions for their upcoming season for kids aged nine to sixteen. My mom said I should try out, and I agreed—to please her. I figured since I loved singing, I'd get in for sure. And for once she'd be proud of me.

She was so happy driving me to the director's studio. I still don't know what she was thinking, letting me go in cold. I mean, she's a professional musician herself. I was only ten years old and didn't really understand what an audition was.

But maybe she thought it was more of a voice-placement thing, because I hadn't been asked to prepare a song. Or maybe she thought the same thing I did. Why *wouldn't* they choose me?

When I went in, I was handed a list of audition songs. I picked "Amazing Grace" because it was the only one I knew. Ms. Winton didn't give me a starting note. She said I should just start singing. So I did. Then she asked me to try it again an octave higher.

My voice went squeaky and flat. I tried again, but now I sounded like a scared cat. I was ready to give it another go, but Ms. Winton said, "Thank you, dear. That will do."

"Please," I begged. "One more try?"

She shook her head and showed me to the door. "I'm sorry, but no. You obviously love to sing, and I admire your enthusiasm, but I can't offer you a place in the Sweetland Singers."

"But," I said, "but my mother—"

"Tell your mother you should take some singing lessons. You need to learn to breathe properly and train your voice."

"And then you'll take me?"

She shook her head. "I'm afraid not. We are a treble choir for girls and for boys whose voices haven't changed. Your range is well below that. Your voice is too low and husky for us." She put her hand on my arm. "But that doesn't mean you shouldn't sing. Follow your passion."

I ran from the studio. My mom was waiting in a room full of other hopeful kids and parents. I held back my tears and smiled.

Instead of the truth, I told my mom it had gone well but that I had decided I didn't want to be in the Sweetland Singers after all.

She tried to make me change my mind. Which made things worse. I never got up the nerve to admit that Ms. Winton didn't want me. And my mom's never gotten over my supposedly turning the Sweetland Singers down.

The memory fades, and I'm back in my room. What if I can never get over my stage fright?

My phone rings. It's Jasmeer. "Great news," she says. "Maxine agreed to coach you! You have an hour with her on Saturday afternoon. Be here at two."

Three

'm thrilled that Maxine Gaston has agreed to work with me. But I'm also scared to death. By Saturday I'm a hot mess of nerves. I want to cancel, but I feel like I have to go through with it.

When I met Maxine at Thanksgiving dinner, she seemed more like a family member than a guest. Or a celebrity. She was humble and easy to talk to. She told me about working with Denzi on the music for *The Lost Song Galaxy* and how nice Denzi is.

But that was with Jasmeer and her parents. This will just be Maxine and me. Well, her and me and my stage fright.

I hum to warm up my voice as I walk over to Jasmeer's place. A new tune drifts around in my head, distracting me with possibilities. Maybe I'll write some lyrics for it later. But when I finally get to Jasmeer's house, my new song floats away.

Fear surges back.

I can't do this.

But I can't *not* do this. Most kids would jump at the chance. I'd be crazy to cancel. I'll never forgive myself if I don't at least try.

Except...what happens when Maxine Gaston asks me to sing?

And what happens if she finds out I didn't actually sign up for *Farmshine*?

My legs turn to jelly as I ring the doorbell.

Sunita, Jasmeer's mom, answers. "Paisley! So good to see you," she says, hugging me. "Jasmeer's in the study."

Jasmeer is busy making her cards for the Farmer's Market. I desperately want to tell her that I need to cancel my session with Maxine. But what comes out is, "Those are definitely going to sell like crazy."

"Thanks," says Jasmeer, not looking up as she carefully positions a photo onto a blank note card. "Excited about your session?"

"Ooh, what are those?" I point to a plate of cookies cut and iced to look like sunflowers.

"My dad's test batch for the bake sale," Jasmeer says. "Help yourself."

I know better than to eat anything now. "I'll grab one later," I say. "They look delish. I love that your dad is contributing!"

"We're all doing our part," Jasmeer says. *Except me*, I think.

Sunita pops her head into the study. "Okay, Paisley," she says. "Maxine is ready for you now."

"Mom," Jasmeer says. "Quit acting like her personal assistant."

Sunita waves her hand at Jasmeer. "Oh, stop it, you. I'm just trying to be helpful." She grabs the plate of cookies and motions for me to follow her.

Jasmeer rolls her eyes. "She is totally starstruck. Have fun! I can't wait to hear all about it."

I follow Sunita to the B&B part of the house. "I knew there was a good reason I put that piano in the guest lounge!" she says. "Luckily, we don't have any other guests checking in today, so you shouldn't be disturbed."

Maxine is at the piano, playing Denzi's "Somewhere the Music Shines Bright." The song I had hoped to sing at *Farmshine*. Does she remember me telling her it's my favorite song?

JOCELYN SHIPLEY

"Paisley's here, Maxine," Sunita says, placing the cookies on a table between a big comfy chair and the sofa.

Maxine stops playing and stands to greet me. She's tall and hip, in jeans and a black turtleneck, her hair in a topknot. "Hello, Paisley," she says, her voice rich and resonant, with just a hint of a French accent. "Nice to see you again."

"Thank you, Ms. Gaston." She's not pretty, like Denzi. She's what people call "interesting looking," with strong features. Kind of like me.

"I'll leave you to it," Sunita says. "But I'll be in the kitchen if you need anything."

So this is it. I need to apologize to Maxine for wasting her time. Get out of here before I throw up. "Ms. Gaston, I really appreciate this, but—"

"Please, call me Maxine. And stop fretting. I'm not going to ask you to sing today."

"You're not?"

"No. Today I want to hear more about you and how I can help."

Whew! The relief is so huge, I almost faint. "Oh! Okay, I guess."

"Let's sit." Maxine settles into the chair.

I pour myself a glass of water from the pitcher next to the plate of cookies. Then I sit on the sofa and take a sip. It helps, so I take another.

"Always good to stay hydrated," Maxine says, reaching for a cookie. "Mmm, so good. Craig is an amazing baker. And Sunita, well, she makes living here a real pleasure. Honestly, I don't know how I'm going to leave when my home renovations are done."

"Yeah, Riverside House is awesome."

Maxine finishes her cookie. "Now, tell me about your singing. Ever had any lessons?"

I shake my head. "I thought about it once, but then, well, it just didn't happen." That awful audition. So humiliating.

Maxine shrugs. "It doesn't necessarily matter. Lots of popular singers are self-taught and don't even read music. Anyway, Jasmeer tells me you're going to sing at *Farmshine*?"

"Well, I want to. But I have this problem with stage fright."

Plus, I'm a total fraud for not signing up.

Maxine reaches for another cookie. "Okay, let's talk about that. First, I want you to name it. Call it what it is—performance anxiety. Second,

I want you to know that performance anxiety is common and manageable. You can learn to accept it as a challenge, rather than a threat, and channel it into performance *energy.*"

Wow. She makes it sound like there is hope after all. "But what if I can't?"

"If you want to succeed in show business, you will."

Her stern tone indicates she won't tolerate me wimping out and feeling sorry for myself. "Okay," I say. "But do you really think I can do this?"

"Of course. That's why I agreed to coach you. Trust me—I've been there and know how hard it can be."

"Seriously?"

"Yes. Performance anxiety can happen to the most experienced performers. Suddenly, out of the blue, you panic. Your mouth goes dry, your heart starts racing, and you think you're going to die."

Maxine pours herself some water and takes a long drink. "I'm going to tell you something you may find hard to believe. I actually found it hard to go from film, where you can always do a

22

retake, back to live theater, where you can't," she says. "Things got so bad for me at one point that I almost quit."

"Really? So what did you do?"

"I had to face my fear and admit I had a problem. And then I went back to basics."

"And those would be?"

"It all starts with proper breathing."

"You mean, like, just take a deep breath?"

"As long as you're doing it properly. Have you ever heard of something called diaphragmatic breathing? It's also called belly breathing or deep breathing."

"Um, maybe? But not exactly, no."

"Shallow breathing won't help you relax, and it doesn't help you sing well. But deep breathing will calm you and give you a supported sound." Maxine stands and places one hand on her stomach. "Like this. First exhale with a big sigh to get rid of all your air. Then, when you breathe in, take air into your belly."

"Shouldn't the air go into my lungs?"

"It will, but focus on expanding the belly instead. Let it fill like a balloon. Breathe through your nose, not your mouth." She demonstrates.

"In for a count of ten...then out for ten." She smiles and says, "Okay, now you try. Stand up."

I feel silly at first. But once I get going, I start to relax.

"You're getting it," Maxine says. "I want you to practice at home every day and come back next week."

"That's it? Just practice breathing?"

"Do five sets in a row, several times a day, and work your way up to ten." Maxine slides onto the piano bench and starts playing softly again.

I guess the lesson is over. "Thanks so, so much!" I say, heading out the door.

"You're welcome," she calls after me. "And don't worry. You'll be fine."

I happy-dance down the hall to the study. "Oh my god, that was fantastic!" I tell Jasmeer. "Maxine is sooooo awesome!"

"Yeah, I know," Jasmeer says. "But my mom being celebrity obsessed is quite enough."

"No worries. It's not like she's Denzi. But somehow Maxine made me feel like I can do anything!"

Like signing up to sing at *Farmshine*.

Four

At the next planning meeting, Vanessa announces that the Sweetland Singers will not be performing at the fundraiser. Everyone groans in disappointment.

Well, everyone but me. I think that's great! Now I have no excuse not to sign up.

Cadence, who is sitting behind Jasmeer and me, strides to the front of the room. "Ms. Winton, our director, asked me to offer our sincere apologies," she says. "We really want to be there, but unfortunately, we were already booked for that night." She pauses for dramatic effect. Then she gazes out at Heath with a lovey-girlfriend look and says, "But we are going to make a big donation to the Save Sunflower Farm fund instead."

Of course she makes it sound like she is personally donating the money.

"Thank you, Cade," Vanessa says, then continues. "I do have some good news about our lineup. As you know, we are still in need of a big name to close the show. And guess what?" She does a little twirly dance. "I've just heard back from Maxine Gaston. Our MC has agreed to sing for us!"

Everyone cheers. When the room settles down, Cadence, desperate for attention as usual, says, "You're all going to love Maxine! I took her class in musical theater for teens last summer, and she is totally amazing!" Then it hits her. "I can't believe I won't be at *Farmshine* to see her. But the Sweetland Singers come first, of course."

I'm sure Cadence wants to keep talking, but Vanessa isn't finished yet. "We now have a fabulous promotional poster, designed by the talented Jasmeer Sharma-Smith," she says. "And our Facebook events page is up and running too. We'll be posting new stuff every day, so be sure to check there for updates. And pick up some posters on your way out. We want to see them all over town."

I pull up the page on my tablet. "Cool," I say to Jasmeer. "I love the sunflower logo. You did a great job."

"Thanks! And you're going to do a great job singing."

"And you know this because?"

"Because you're working on your stage fright."

My stomach clenches. "Performance anxiety. Anyway, working on it doesn't mean I'll actually get over it." And I still haven't signed up.

Too late, I realize Cadence has come back to her seat right behind us. Uh-oh. Was she listening in? I really hope not.

"Okay, so let's hear from the committees," Vanessa says. The kids in charge of the program, publicity, donations, decorations, tickets, intermission sales and after-party for the cast and crew all give their reports. Before closing the meeting, Vanessa makes one last call for performers.

This is it. I have to sign up. I find the kid with the clipboard and add my name to the talent sheet. When I turn to leave, Cadence is blocking my way.

She smirks and says, "That's brave of you."

"What do you mean?" I try to step around her.

Cadence moves in front of me again. "I mean, with your stage fright, you're really taking a chance, aren't you?" It's not exactly a question.

Great. She *did* hear. "Well, Maxine says I'll be fine."

"Maxine?"

"Yeah, you know, our MC. I'm getting personal coaching from her."

"*Maxine Gaston* is coaching you?" Cadence looks stunned. "Really?"

"Really."

"I don't believe you."

"Well, I had an hour-long session with her on Saturday, and I'm going back next week."

"But," Cadence says, "I don't understand. I begged her to take me after that summer thing. She said she *never* does private coaching."

I shrug. "Well, she agreed to coach me." Even though I didn't have the nerve to sign up for her summer thing.

"I don't believe you. If she was going to take anybody, it would be me. I excelled in her class."

"Well..." I smirk at her like she did at me. "Guess she made an exception."

Cadence shakes her head. "You're lying."

"I'm not."

"Okay then. Where do you have these sessions?"

"Sorry, can't tell you." No one is supposed to know that Maxine is staying at Riverside House. They don't want fans stalking her or whatever. The fact that me keeping it secret drives Cadence nuts is just a bonus.

"Riiiiiiight," says Cadence. "You can't tell me because you made the whole thing up. You can't even sing."

Whatever. I turn to walk away from her but she's got more to say. "I know you auditioned for the Sweetland Singers when you moved here," she says.

Oh my god! How much does she know?

"I auditioned that day too," she says. "You went up right before me. But you didn't get in. I could tell by the fake smile on your face."

"Actually, she did offer me a place, but I changed my mind." *Now* I was lying. I couldn't help it.

Cadence gasps. "Totally not true! Nobody turns down a place in the Sweetland Singers."

"Well, *I* did. I'm more of a solo performer." What am I doing? Can I dig myself in any deeper?

But she's making me so mad. "And yeah, I can sing, all right. I've done *lots* of singing."

Cadence bursts out laughing. "I hope you don't mean with the Stonehill Elementary School Choir?"

Great. I tried to join the school choir to make my mom happy after the Sweetland disaster. You didn't have to audition; you just had to love to sing. I'd forgotten Cadence was in that choir too, so she knows how that worked out. "No, of course not. I sing all the time by myself." Could I sound any more pathetic?

"Okaaay," Cadence says. "But all the other performers have a lot of experience. Some of them are even semiprofessional. So you might want to reconsider."

I hate her so much. She's in the Sweetland Singers, she's going with the guy I like, and she's my main competition for our school musical next term. Not that a ninth-grader could ever land a lead role, but you never know.

"Thanks for the advice, but I'll definitely be singing at *Farmshine*."

"Well then." Cadence does her hair flip thing. "I can't wait to hear how you do!"

Five

Gah! What have I done? I signed up even though I'm scared to sing in public. Even though I failed my first and only audition. Even though I've never taken any singing lessons.

Yeah, I have a famous coach to help me. But I landed her by sheer luck. And she's never even heard me sing.

Why'd I go and brag to Cadence? Now she'll tell everybody I claim to be working with Maxine Gaston. And they'll all expect me to be terrific. And just because the Sweetland Singers won't be there doesn't mean I'll be able to manage onstage.

And then there's my mother. She might be happy I want to sing, but she'll disapprove of my choosing a Denzi song. What have I let myself in for? It's twenty-five days until *Farmshine*, and I'm going to spend every one of them worrying.

I'm surprised to see my mother's car in the driveway when I get home. Just what I need. No chance of grabbing some cold pizza and avoiding her. She's already making dinner. "Hey, you're early," I say. "What's up?"

"A student canceled a lesson." She stirs a pot of tomato sauce. "And you're late. Where were you?"

"Planning meeting. Remember I told you about that fundraiser for Sunflower Farm?" I take a poster from my backpack and unroll it to show her. I plan to keep it forever as a souvenir of my debut. It will probably become a collector's item.

"Ah, of course." She tastes the sauce and adds a shake of sea salt. "I hope they make a lot of money."

"Yeah, me too. Isn't the poster great? Jasmeer designed it. And she took this photo!"

"Impressive! That girl's got talent." My mother turns down the heat to let the sauce simmer. "And what are you going to do?"

I can't look at her. "I'll probably be backstage or something." Not a complete lie. "Are you planning to go?"

She glances at the poster again. "Oh, sorry, I can't. I have a student recital that night. I mean, if would be different if you were in the program."

"Yeah." Technically, I'm *not* in the program. They haven't been printed yet.

"I'll make a donation though." She puts water on to boil for the pasta. "Can you set the table?"

"Sure." Maybe I'll never have to tell her. My dad plays hockey on Friday nights, so he probably won't want to go either. And if neither of them are there, maybe she'll never know.

After dinner I click on the *Farmshine* Facebook page again. Jasmeer's photos of the limestone farmhouse, sunflower fields and vegetable stand really show what a special place Sunflower Farm is.

The latest post is an updated list of performers. I scan the names and see mine at the very bottom. There are already a hundred likes and even some comments, mostly about what a great show it's going to be.

And then there's this one. *Yay! Paisley McFarland is such a good singer!*

Whoa! Somebody likes my singing? I like it right away, without checking who made the comment.

But then I realize in horror that it was posted by @CadenceWang. The profile picture is a selfie of Cadence and Heath.

Why would Cadence say something like that? It would make sense if she'd dissed me. But being supportive? What's going on?

Then my phone buzzes with a text. **Joke! U sing like a stuck pig.**

Cadence must have been waiting until she knew I'd seen her comment. But how did she even get my number?

I can't stop myself from replying **Do not!**

Cadence: **Right, forgot. U r scared to sing at all!**

Me: **Shut up!**

Cadence: **Stage fright!**

Me: **No problem thanx to Maxine G!**

Cadence: **She cant help u! Because stage fright!!!**

Me: **She picked me not u. Jealous much?**

Cadence: **No! U r jealous of me & Heath.**

How does she know I have a crush on her boyfriend? I've never told anybody, not even Jasmeer. But it's probably obvious to Cadence. Girls like her know these things.

There's no way to reply. She's right. I *am* jealous. I turn off my phone and go to bed.

But I can't sleep. What if my mother checks the Facebook page? She might have noticed the link on the poster. Not that she uses Facebook much. She likes social media about as much as she likes Denzi.

Still, if she's going to find out, it should be from me. On the other hand, why tell her until I'm sure I'm over my stage fright? No use getting into a fight over nothing.

The next day I wait for Jasmeer at her locker. As soon as she gets there I show her the comment and texts from Cadence.

"You gave her your number?" Jasmeer asks. "Why would you do that?"

"I didn't. She must have copied it from my contact info on the sign-up sheet."

Jasmeer hangs up her coat and checks her hair in her mirror. "Delete the texts and block her number. She's just trying to intimidate you."

"But why?"

"Because she's worried Heath likes you? I've heard she's pretty possessive."

"He doesn't even know I exist."

"So maybe she's jealous of you having coaching with Maxine? Here, hold this. I can't find my binder." She hands me her backpack.

"Okay, jealous of Maxine makes more sense," I say. "But what I don't get is why she'd pretend to be nice to me on Facebook."

"I don't know. Maybe she's hoping to make you mess up onstage."

"What? How?"

"By making everybody's expectations so high you can never live up to them?" Jasmeer stuffs her binder in her backpack, shuts her locker and heads for class.

I walk along with her. "Maybe. Cadence *is* super competitive."

"And she's trying to cover herself. Nobody will believe anything bad about her when she's so publicly supportive of you."

"I guess. So what do I do?"

"Ignore her," Jasmeer says. "Focus on your singing. Breathe."

Six

I take Jasmeer's advice and practice instead of obsessing about Cadence. By Saturday when I arrive for my second coaching session with Maxine, I'm feeling upbeat and confident.

Jasmeer and her mom are busy with B&B chores, so today it's Maxine who greets me. She looks striking in a purple silk tunic over black leggings, her salt and pepper hair in a wrap-around braid. I love how confident she is in her personal style. Something else I need to work on.

The house smells of apples and cinnamon. "Care for some mulled cider?" she asks.

"Yes, please!"

Maxine brings two mugs into the lounge. She's used candy canes for stir sticks.

I take a sip of my cider and then set my mug on the coffee table. "So, Maxine, I heard you're going to sing your Silver Spinner song at *Farmshine*. That's beyond cool! And you're way more famous than the Sweetland Singers, so we'll sell way more tickets."

Maxine laughs. "Enough with the flattery," she says. "Time to get to work."

After a few rounds of deep breathing, she says, "Okay, let's warm up your voice." She goes to the piano and hits a note. "Up and down the scale from there. Don't forget to breathe from your belly."

I'm so awed by Maxine that I forget to be afraid. I take a deep breath and open my mouth. My voice, already warmed up because of my singing as I walked over to Jasmeer's, comes out clear and strong.

"Impressive," Maxine says. "Paisley, I believe you have what we call raw talent."

Is that a good thing? "Um, what does that mean exactly?"

"It means I think you definitely have what it takes to be a very good singer."

Definitely a good thing. "Wow, thanks! My dream is to be a pop singer, like Denzi. But my mom is disappointed that I don't want to sing Italian arias."

Maxine lifts her hands off the keys and tilts her head. "Is that where your performance anxiety comes from?"

I sip some more of my cider. "Yeah—but only part of it."

"Go on."

"I had a really bad audition once," I say. "So there's that too."

"What happened?"

"A few years ago I tried out for the Sweetland Singers."

Maxine sits up straighter on the piano bench. "And?"

"And it was a total disaster." By the time I've finished telling her the whole story, I'm close to tears.

"Okay now, breathe," Maxine says. "Use the technique to calm yourself."

I try, but I end up gulping like a beached fish. Eventually, though, my breathing evens out.

"Paisley, listen to me," says Maxine. "Elaine Winton is a bit of a dragon, but she is fair and she knows her stuff. From what you've told me, it sounds like she was just noting your low vocal range, which is not common in young women. She wasn't saying you weren't any good."

"That's not how it felt."

"So you just gave up?"

"No, I tried to sing with the school choir, but that didn't work out either." Which Cadence so kindly reminded me about. "The teacher made me stand with the boys. But my voice was even lower than most of theirs, and everybody laughed. So, yeah, I guess I gave up."

Maxine raises her eyebrows and shakes her head. "That must have been hard."

"Yeah, it was."

"But you know what? Not many women *can* sing in that range. I certainly can't. So try thinking of it as a positive rather than a negative. You don't have a conventional female voice. And you have star power."

"I *do*?"

"Absolutely. But that raw talent needs to be developed." She gets up from the piano, takes a sip of her cider, then returns to the piano. "Everybody has unsuccessful auditions. You have to learn to get past failure. You have to take control of your performance anxiety." She plays a few notes, then asks, "What do you think is the worst that could happen onstage?"

I freeze. I can't think about being onstage without panicking. I have to belly-breathe before I can answer. "I guess my greatest fear is that the words won't come out and the audience will heckle me and someone will have to drag me offstage. Or maybe I'll start singing and forget the words. I've seen that happen on those *Idol* shows on TV. And then it gets posted on YouTube."

"But it doesn't have to," Maxine says. "It's all about respecting your audience. They've paid good money to be there, so you need to be very well rehearsed. You need to practice until you know your notes and lyrics cold. That way, no matter what distractions pop up, you can keep singing on autopilot."

"Wouldn't singing on autopilot be bad?"

"Not as bad as losing your place. The goal is to know your stuff so well, nothing can make you lose focus and blank out."

"Okay," I say.

"Let's give it a try." Maxine plays the intro of my song, motioning with her head that I should come and stand near the piano. I move closer, exhale, take a deep breath and come in right on time.

"Excellent!" Maxine claps her hands. "I love how your voice is so different from Denzi's. It almost sounds like a new song. As they say on those *Idol* shows, you really made it your own."

"Thanks!" I feel like I sang it better than I ever have. "But it's just you and me here. It's going to be totally different at *Farmshine*."

"Not totally," Maxine says. "I'll be there to introduce and accompany you. Try to capture the confidence you're feeling *right now* so you can tap into that feeling when you're up onstage."

"Yeah, but all those people in the audience—"

"Want to be entertained. They're on your side. They want you to be great."

"I guess." But not everybody. Not Cadence.

"You're going to focus on the singing, not the fear. All your anxiety will be transformed into excitement and confidence. You're going to stride out there with pride and power and a great big smile. You're going to take command of the stage, acknowledge the audience, grab them by the throat from the first note and not let them go until the last one."

"You make it sound so easy!" I laugh, giddy with relief. I sang for Maxine, and she didn't make fun of me. She didn't say I was wasting her time. She didn't say she was done coaching me.

"It's all about being prepared." Maxine checks her watch and stands, pushing the bench back under the piano. "Keep practicing with proper breathing, and I'll see you next week."

"Thank you, thank you, thank you."

"You're most welcome." Maxine gives me a big smile. "Your interpretation could use some more dynamics, and we can talk more about that next time. Sing at *Farmshine* like you just did and you'll have people lining up for your autograph."

Seven

I find Jasmeer in the laundry room of Riverside House. "Maxine is the best!" I squeal. "She's helping me so much! And she just called my singing excellent!"

"Cool!" Jasmeer stacks some towels into a basket. "I hope you're feeling better about going onstage."

"Yeah, I think I am. I'm still a bit nervous, but—"

"You're going to be awesome! Now, want to help me scrub a couple of bathrooms?"

"Ha! Not a chance." I check my phone, which I had turned off while working with Maxine.

Great. Cadence has sent another text. This one's got a picture attached. There's my face, from my student ID, photoshopped onto a pig's body. **Pissley McFartland is gonna stink at Farmshine!**

I stare in shock, then hold my phone out to Jasmeer.

She takes a look and gasps. "Oh my god! That's disgusting!"

My phone buzzes. Cadence again. **Pissley McFatland sings like oink, oink, oink!**

"You don't need this," Jasmeer says. "Block her number."

Before I can do that, Cadence sends another picture. This one shows my head on a full-figured opera singer's body. My very large chest is bursting out of my dress, which has the name *Pissley McFatland* scrawled across it.

Is that supposed to be an insult? I may not want to be an opera singer, but thanks to my mom, I appreciate how talented they are. This is so childish.

"Maybe you should report her or something," Jasmeer says.

"Yeah, maybe." I know I should ignore her. But again, I can't help but reply. **Pls stop.**

Cadence: **Never over till the fat lady sings!**

Me: **Maxine G says I'm excellent!**

Cadence: **Major stage fright!!!**

I turn off my phone again.

I usually sing to myself as I walk home. But now I'm too distracted. About Cadence, yes, but I'm also feeling bad about keeping my parents in the dark. They don't even know I'm planning to perform.

By the time I get home, I've decided I really need to tell them.

I get my chance at dinner. They both seem to be in good moods.

"Great veggie burgers, Mom," I say. "And Dad, these sweet-potato fries are the best." I pass the green salad I made. "Oh, and by the way, I signed up to sing at *Farmshine.*"

Dad stops spooning salad onto his plate. My mother stops eating, her fork halfway to her mouth. There's an awkward silence.

"What's *Farmshine?*" asks Dad.

I fill him in, and then Mom asks, "What song are you singing?"

I speak to the fry dangling from her fork. "It's called 'Somewhere the Music Shines Bright.' You know—the theme from *The Lost Song Galaxy* movie?"

"No, I don't know." Mom points her fork at Dad, making the fry fall off onto her plate. "Do you know it?"

Dad passes the salad along. "Sure, it was a big hit when that movie came out. I think Denzi wrote and recorded it, didn't she, Paisley?"

"That's right," I say, impressed that my dad knows. "She actually wrote the entire movie score. That song is my favorite. It starts out all dark and minor and harsh, and then the chorus is lyrical and hopeful, because the movie's about finding music that's been lost. And I sing it really well—Maxine even said so."

"Maxine?" my parents ask together.

Oops. I never told them about the coaching either. I was worried Mom would forbid it. "Yeah, um, you know, Maxine Gaston? The Stratford actor? She was in *The Lost Song Galaxy* movie, and she's the MC for the fundraiser."

"I've certainly heard of her," Mom says. "But when did she hear you sing?"

I explain how Jasmeer set it all up. "It's kind of vocal coaching, but it's really more about helping me get over my stage fright. And if I can manage to sing at *Farmshine*, then I'll be able to audition for the school musical next term." Might as well tell her everything and put a positive spin on it. "Can you believe it? I'm so incredibly lucky to have this chance."

Mom stares at me. "You have performance anxiety?"

I can't tell her about failing the Sweetland Singers audition, because she thinks I turned it down. I can't tell her about the school choir either, because she doesn't even know I tried out for it. "Lots of singers have stage fright."

"Yes, I'm well aware of that," Mom says. "Every performer has to deal with nerves."

"Not you. You always seem so calm before a concert." Which is why I can't talk to her about it.

Mom shrugs. "I guess I'm lucky that way, but it certainly helps that I'm not a soloist. I'm never alone onstage. I have the whole symphony around me." She serves herself some salad. "But back to you. You haven't been singing anywhere, so I don't understand."

"I sing in private, when you're not here," I say. "So you won't get upset. Because we don't like the same kind of music. And when I think about performing onstage, I have something like a panic attack."

"Oh." She raises her eyebrows at me. "Well, maybe if you'd joined the Sweetland Singers, the director would have been able to help you."

Thanks, Mom! "But I don't want to sing that kind of music. I don't want to be part of a choir. I want to be a pop singer."

Mom opens her mouth to speak, then closes it again. Maybe she's trying to stop herself from saying the wrong thing.

"Sorry," I say. "But I'm going to do a Denzi song."

Mom stabs another fry with her fork. "Hmm. Up to you. But I won't be able to be there. As I said, I have a student recital that night."

"That's okay." The last thing I want or need is my mother in the audience.

"I'll be there," Dad says. "Even if your mom is too embarrassed to hear you sing a pop song."

Mom ignores Dad's attempt at teasing. This isn't funny to her. The conversation is over and the subject is closed.

After dinner I put the kettle on. When the water boils, I pour it over a mint tea bag and carry it to my room.

I shut the door, plunk down on my bed and stare at the walls. I painted them over the summer—one purple, one yellow, one green and one pink. Kind of like the streaks in my hair.

The walls are covered with posters of Denzi in concert. On my dresser is a photo of Mom in the long black dress she wears for playing with the symphony. I'm so envious of her ease onstage. I wish she'd given me some tips on how to deal with things. But all she did was make me feel guilty about not joining the Sweetland Singers.

Time to rehearse. I run through "Somewhere the Music Shines Bright" five times. But I don't want to overdo it. Maxine said all I had to do was sing it like I did today.

But what if I can never sing it that well again?

Eight

I t's a long week at school. I've blocked Cadence from my phone, and I try to avoid her. But every time I do see her in class or the hall, she whispers, "Hey, Pissley." Or "Hey, McFatland." Then she makes *oink, oink* sounds at me.

I want to scream, but that might damage my vocal cords. What is her problem?

Whatever it is, I can't let her rattle me.

When I arrive for my next coaching session, Maxine is playing the piano and singing "The Universe Is Made of Music." That's her song from the movie and is the one she'll perform at *Farmshine*. It's the first time I've heard her sing in person. I'm blown away by her powerful voice, which fills the room. She nods at me and says between bars, "Please join in, if you know it."

If I know it? It's a Denzi song—of course I do! I come in on the chorus, harmonizing with Maxine.

The sound of our voices together is amazing. After Maxine plays the final notes, I have no words. And even if I did, saying anything right now would ruin the moment.

Maxine is also quiet. Eventually she says, "I haven't sung that in a long while. I'd forgotten how much I like it. And I especially liked us singing it together."

"Oh, me too!" I say. "I mean, I like the song, and it was a huge honor to sing it with you!"

Maxine nods and flows right into my *Farmshine* song. After I've run through it, she gives me some specific tips on how I can improve. I sing it again and again, until she says, "Bravo! Let's leave it there for today. I have something else I want you to work on."

She gets up from the piano and moves over to the armchair. "So, Paisley, tell me. Are you feeling ready?"

"Um, maybe? I really know the song and the breathing. But I still panic when I think about going onstage."

"Yes, I suspected that. Have you ever heard of visualization?"

"Maybe?"

"Well, visualization is picturing an image to help you reach a goal. Let's give it a go. I'm going to lead you through your performance, from start to finish. Sit on the sofa, close your eyes, and try to clear your mind."

I try, but my thoughts are all over the place. I'm still high on the joy of my duet with Maxine. I do some deep breathing, but it takes a while before I can say, "Ready."

"Okay," Maxine says. "Picture this. You're in the wings, about to perform. You look great and know your song perfectly. You're controlling your nerves with your breathing. No matter what's happening around you, you're not distracted. Nothing can make you lose focus. You saw the stage at sound-check, so you know exactly where you'll stand, where the mic is and how to use it. You're ready for the bright lights shining right in your eyes."

I'm so there. Maxine's words help me picture everything.

"I introduce you to a full house," she says. "You stride out and take command of the stage, full of confidence. You flash your smile and acknowledge the audience, connecting with them immediately. As I start to play your song, you stay focused and breathe."

I can almost hear her playing the opening bars.

"You hit the first note right on pitch, just like you always do. You transform every bit of fear into positive energy and emotion, and send it out to the audience. You give them your heart through your music."

This feels totally right. Exactly what I want to do.

"Each phrase you sing is better than the last. You build to the final note, which you hold forever. Because you can. You're that good. When you finally let go, there's silence, then mad applause. You bow graciously. The audience gives you the standing ovation you deserve."

I open my eyes, almost expecting to see the audience on their feet. "Oh my god! That was awesome! Do you really think I can do that?"

Maxine nods.

"So I'm guessing my homework this week is to practice visualization?"

"It's a powerful tool. Go over and over the details. That will ensure you're ready for the next step."

"Next step?"

"There's no dress rehearsal, just a soundcheck the night before. But in order to be certain you have your performance anxiety under control, you need to rehearse in front of a live audience."

"Didn't I just do that?"

"I mean an audience of more than one."

"Oh." Maybe I should have expected that, but I didn't. "So, like, who, exactly?"

"Jasmeer and her parents. Here. Next Saturday. I've already set it up. You'll sing for friends in a comfortable, familiar setting."

I say goodbye and rush to find Jasmeer. She's at the computer in the study. "Hey, I hear you're going to sing for us next week," she says. "That's great!"

"Yeah, I guess. Maxine thinks it's a good idea."

"And you don't?"

"Well, I hope it is. We had a great session today, so I think I'm ready." I glance at the computer screen. "What are you working on?"

"The *Farmshine* program. Want to see?"

"Of course!"

Jasmeer shows me her rough layout. "Great design," I say. But all I'm seeing is the performance order. I'm not on until the second half, which means a lot of super-anxious waiting. But at least I'm on first. I guess you could say I'm opening the second half.

Jasmeer grabs her camera. "Can you go stand over there by the wall and point toward the window?"

"Okay, but why?"

"Promo photos for the Facebook page. We're going to post about the various performers to create buzz and help sell tickets. So I need to take your picture. Oh, and Vanessa's asked me to be the official event photographer."

"Yay you!"

I strike poses while Jasmeer snaps away. It feels weird to point to a window for no reason, but I assume Jasmeer knows what she's doing. "You're going to take photos of everybody in the show?" I ask.

"No, some have their own publicity shots, so we'll use those." Jasmeer sets her camera down. "Okay, that's good. You can relax now, rock star."

We scroll through the photos together. Jasmeer deletes most of them. Then she uploads the best one to the computer for editing.

I peer over her shoulder at the screen. She layers her shot of me onto another picture. Instead of me standing by a wall pointing to the window, it looks like I'm outside, pointing to the town sign:

Welcome to Stonehill. Proud home of hockey legend Hank Rundall, pop star Denzi, and the Sweetland Singers.

"Wow! Way better than Cadence's nasty photoshop efforts!"

We both start to laugh, then stop. What Cadence did wasn't funny.

"Don't worry about her," Jasmeer says. "She's just jealous because you'll have your name up on that sign for real someday."

"Thanks," I say. "But you've never even heard me sing."

"I will next week," she says. "So excited!"

Nine

"Ticket sales are terrific!" Vanessa announces at the next meeting. "We've sold 250 of 400! That's over 60 percent! I have free tickets for all the volunteers, so pick them up before you leave. And tell your family and friends to call the Stonehill Theater box office. Let's make this thing a sold-out event!"

Everybody but me cheers.

Hearing those numbers made me feel faint. That's a big audience. No, a *huge* audience. A huge, scary audience.

I wish this thing was over already! The waiting is torture.

And there's still my practice performance on Saturday. I've been working on picturing it going well. But visualizing is way harder without Maxine's confident words and calming voice.

Maxine warned me about negative thinking, though, so I try to let go of the worrying. I try to pay attention to the meeting. "Jasmeer has posted pictures of all our performers on our Facebook page," Vanessa says. "She's going to be our official event photographer, and I'm going to shoot video. I'm hoping all the performers and their families, plus everyone who can't make the show, will want to buy a copy."

Not my mom. She'll make a donation, but I doubt she'll want to see me singing a Denzi song. I'm pretty sure she could rearrange her schedule. It's not like she'd miss her end-of-year gala.

But it doesn't matter, because I don't want her to come.

As the committees give their reports, I check out the promo photos.

The first one I see is the Sweetland Singers, with Cadence in the center of the front row. I freeze. What's up with that? I thought they weren't available. I thought they weren't performing. But maybe they're on the Facebook page because they're making a big donation?

When I came into the meeting room, I deliberately chose a seat as far from Cadence as possible. Now I turn to glare at her. She's staring at me like she was waiting for me to look over at her. She gives a little wave and flashes me a big, innocent smile.

I go back to the promo photos. I'm surprised at how many kids have their own publicity shots already. And personal websites.

I never even thought about stuff like that. I only thought about singing. And stage fright. Still, Jasmeer's photo of me pointing to the Stonehill sign looks great. I look like a star already. And I can see the picture has got tons of likes. Even some nice comments.

Including this one from Cadence: *Congrats to Stonehill's next celebrity! Paisley McFarland is going to be awesome! Especially now that she's being coached by the great Maxine Gaston, aka Silver Spinner!*

Oh no! I didn't want anybody to know about Maxine. But it's my own stupid fault. Why did I open my big mouth?

"People! Please!" Vanessa has to shout to be heard. "I've got one more amazing announcement!"

Vanessa waits until it's quiet. Until all eyes are off screens and on her. "I am absolutely thrilled to announce that the Sweetland Singers have managed to rearrange their schedule." She pauses and smiles over at Cadence. "They're going to be able to perform at *Farmshine* after all!"

Once again, everybody but me cheers.

Oh my god! I'm doomed!

When things settle down again, Vanessa adds, "I've slotted them in to open the second half of the show, right after intermission."

I suck in my breath. That was my spot! Mine!

"Then Paisley," Vanessa says, looking at me. "You'll be on right after them."

Oh no! That means I'll be waiting in the wings, sweating and shaking. I won't be able to stop myself from reliving that horrible audition. Then I'll have to watch and listen to all those kids like Cadence who *were* good enough for the Sweetland Singers.

And then I'll have to follow their stellar performance.

I try to breathe and remember what Maxine said about Ms. Winton's reasons for turning me down. It's not working.

"You okay?" Jasmeer asks.

A few minutes ago I was set to overcome my stage fright. I was ready to amaze everyone at *Farmshine*. Thanks to Maxine, I believed I had what it takes.

Now all I have is a churning stomach and a pounding heart. I pause a beat too long before saying, "Yeah, why?"

"You don't like the Sweetland Singers?"

"Sure I do." This comes out too fast. But I can't admit how I really feel about them. Not going there. "Everybody likes them."

I make the mistake of looking over at Cadence again. She's beaming like she's the one who made it happen. Like being in the Sweetland Singers is the best thing ever. Which it maybe is. I wouldn't know.

I give her the stink eye.

Heath, sitting beside her, gives me a dirty look back. He must have thought it was meant for him. Great. Now he's going to think I'm an idiot.

I shake my head and point to Cadence.

She pretends to blow me a kiss.

Heath looks back and forth between us. Like, *what's going on here?*

I wish I could go over and tell him I'd never look at him like that. That it's his evil girlfriend making me crazy. But I've got a bigger problem than Cadence.

The Sweetland Singers.

I can't perform after them. I just can't.

There's no use asking Vanessa to change the order. No matter where I am on the program, I'll never get up the nerve to sing if they're there. Just the thought of hearing them makes my throat close up tight.

"You sure you're okay?" Jasmeer says. "You look kind of sick or something."

"I was just thinking about this comment Cadence posted." I point to the page, open on my tablet. "Can you delete it?"

Jasmeer looks puzzled. "I could, but why?"

"It's like she's trying to set me up to fail. The more she says how great a singer I am, the more I feel like I'm not."

"Hmm. I see what you mean, but nobody else knows that. Her comment is great for publicity."

"Please? I don't really want everybody knowing about my coaching with Maxine, either."

"But what would I tell Vanessa? She's already seen and liked it. She would want to know why."

"Oh, right." No way am I making this worse by trying to explain things to Vanessa. "Forget it then." I close my tablet and put it in my backpack. Cadence would only repost her comment anyway. Or something worse.

Ten

I trudge home through the season's first snow-storm. I don't have boots or mitts or a hat, but it doesn't matter. I'm already numb. The Sweetland Singers are performing right before me. What on earth am I going to do?

I make myself a grilled cheese and some hot chocolate. But I'm too upset to eat. And I can't concentrate on homework.

I need to talk to Maxine.

I don't have a meeting booked with her until Saturday, right before I sing for Jasmeer and her parents. But I can't wait that long. I know how busy she is, and I hate to bother her, but she's the only one who really understands.

I don't have her number, so I call Jasmeer. But Maxine is out. Jasmeer says she'll get her to call me later. But I need help now, before I totally lose it.

I know what would she tell me to do. Calm myself with deep breathing. I try to clear my mind and focus on controlling my air flow. Exhale. Drop diaphragm. Inhale. Hold. Repeat. And it does work. A bit.

Singing will help even more. I put Denzi's *Greatest Hits* on my iPod and rock out. Then I run through my song several times, working on phrasing, dynamics and vocal production. I sing my heart out to my favorite poster of Denzi.

I'm feeling so much better, I decide to do my visualization exercise. I sit cross-legged on my bed, close my eyes and imagine it's the night of the show.

I'm waiting in the wings, listening to the Sweetland Singers. They're really good, but I don't let that bother me. I'm ready to sing, and I'm going to nail it. But then Ms. Winton looks over and sees me. She stops the choir and turns to address the audience. "I'm sorry, but there's a girl backstage who shouldn't be here. She auditioned for me, and certainly wasn't good enough to join my fabulous choir. She's a terrible singer!"

Yikes! That wasn't supposed to happen. I really need to talk to Maxine. I hope she calls back soon.

I wipe the image of Ms. Winton from my mind and try again. This time I skip ahead to my grand entrance.

I'm wearing a terrific outfit, and my hair looks amazing. The audience is screaming, "Paisley! Paisley! Paisley!" as I stride onstage. My smile is radiant, my arms outstretched to acknowledge the applause. I'm ready for the bright lights that almost blind me. Maxine plays my intro, and I hear my starting note. But then I glance down at the front row, and there's my mom. I start to sing anyway, but she rushes onstage in her long black symphony dress and announces, "My daughter is such a disappointment!"

What's going on? Why can't I get through this in a positive way? Is it going to keep getting harder to visualize success the closer I get to performance night?

I can't leave that image of Mom in my head. I walk it back and try again.

I've made my powerful entrance and I'm singing beautifully, really connecting with the audience. But then someone throws a rotten tomato.

It splats on the floor at my feet. I ignore it. Maxine nods encouragement from the piano. Keep going, don't let anything distract you. *But then another tomato comes flying through the air and hits my shoulder. Bright red juice runs down my sleeve. Another hits me smack on the forehead. As I wipe tomato juice from my face, I hear Cadence's voice.* "You suck big-time, Pissley McFatland!"

Right. Okay then. Visualization is definitely not working. I go and dump my uneaten sandwich in the green bin and pour my hot chocolate down the sink. I'm loading the dishwasher when Mom gets home.

"Whew, it's really snowing," she says. "The roads are terrible." She steps out of her boots and hangs up her coat. "How was your day, sweetheart?"

She's been extra nice since I told her about performing at *Farmshine*. Maybe because she's making an effort to hide her disapproval of my song choice.

"Okay." Which is not true at all. But I don't want to get into it. "How was yours?"

"Same as always," she says. "Busy, busy, busy." She fills the kettle with water and switches it on.

"I need nice hot tea. Want some?"

"No, thanks, I had hot chocolate already." I wish I could have tea with Mom and tell her everything. From that horrible audition to the ugly images Cadence sent me. But the conversation will probably turn into her trying to convince me not to do a Denzi song. Or reminding me that pop music is inferior. "I think I'll just go to bed early. I walked home, and I'm exhausted."

"Paisley, are you okay?" Mom's voice sounds full of concern. "You're not coming down with something, are you? Why on earth did you walk home on such a miserable day?"

"There was a *Farmshine* meeting, and I missed the bus. And anyway, I like walking." And I needed to clear my head.

"Okay, well, you need to take care of yourself. Maybe getting to bed early is a good idea." Mom turns off the boiling kettle and makes her tea. "Oh, by the way, I saw Elaine Winton in the grocery store, and she told me the Sweetland Singers are going to perform at *Farmshine*."

Wait. What? I busy myself rearranging the dishwasher so Mom won't see the shock on my face. "You know Ms. Winton?"

"Not personally," Mom says. "But I do know her professionally. She's on the Symphony Board this year, and we both belong to Women of Note."

"Oh." Have they ever talked about my audition? Would Ms. Winton even remember me? "Yeah, Vanessa said at the meeting today that the Sweetland Singers would be there."

Mom adds some honey to her tea. "You know," she says, "I still think it's a shame you never joined that choir."

Here we go. "Mom! That was years ago! I don't want to talk about it."

"Okay, but Elaine told me she's planning to start a youth choir next year, just for older kids. Maybe you could audition for that?"

Seriously? When will she get it? "I don't think so, Mom. It's really not for me." I finish cleaning up. "I think I'm off to bed now. Good night."

"Sleep well. Oh! I almost forgot to tell you! I moved things around so I can come see the show."

There's a beat before I can even speak. "You did?"

"Yes. But that's certainly not the reaction I was expecting. I thought you'd be happy."

"Oh, yeah, I am. Just surprised is all." And wondering how this magically happened right after she talked to Ms. Winton.

"I'll get Dad to buy two tickets," she says as we share an awkward goodnight hug.

Perfect. Just perfect. And after she's blown away by the Sweetland Singers, she can watch me try to sing Denzi's best song. Which I'll probably screw up, because my disapproving mom is in the audience. "Great," I say. "It's going to be a fabulous show."

Eleven

At lunch the next day, Jasmeer passes me a container of cookies. "My dad is still trying to perfect his sunflower design," she says. "What do you think?"

I study them for a minute. "Hmm. I like the green leaf he added, but it looks like it would be a lot more work to mass-produce them."

"Exactly what he figured out," Jasmeer says. "You can have them."

"All of them? Thanks!" I grab one and take a big bite.

"Yup. I can't eat any more." She chooses an apple instead. "Oh, hey, I meant to ask. Can you help with cookie sales at intermission?"

I almost choke. "No!" I take a drink. "I mean, sorry, but I can't."

"Why not? It would take your mind off going onstage in the second half."

"But Maxine said that during intermission I should find a quiet place, block out everything, do some deep breathing and focus on my performance."

"Oh," Jasmeer says. "Okay, that makes sense."

"And speaking of Maxine, did you give her my message?" I waited and waited last night, but she didn't call.

Jasmeer pats my arm. "She was still out when I went to bed, so I put a note under her door," she says. "Don't worry—she'll call. And you're going to be fine. You know that, right?"

No. I'll probably be throwing up in the washroom at intermission. That's if I'm still going to sing. "I *don't* know, actually. Maybe I should go find Vanessa right now and take my name off the list."

"Whoa! Don't say that. Don't even think it!"

"Well, it's hard not to imagine the worst. I mean, the Sweetland Singers are on right before me."

"Huh? So what?"

I didn't mean to mention them. But now I can't stop myself from telling Jasmeer the story

of my failed audition. She listens without inter-
rupting. When I'm done she says, "But that was
years ago. And isn't Maxine helping you work
through your anxiety? I thought you said your
coaching was going great."

"Yeah, it is. But—"

Just then a group of girls surrounds us. Girls
who've never spoken to me before. They're all
talking at once.

"Hey, are you Paisley?"

"Are you the girl Maxine Gaston is coaching?"

"You must be really good!"

"Can't wait to hear you sing!"

They must have seen Cadence's post. My
mouth goes dry and my legs go wobbly. "Let's
get out of here," I say to Jasmeer. We pack up
our lunch stuff and try to escape. But the girls
follow us.

"How'd you get Maxine to coach you?"

"What's it like working with her?"

Jasmeer turns and faces the pack. "Paisley
has no statement to make at this time. Please
respect her privacy."

"Thanks," I say, the two of us laughing as we
exit the cafeteria. "You're hired."

"Done. And my advice as your new manager? Forget everything but your singing."

"I know," I say. "I'll try."

* * *

It's after nine o'clock when I finally hear from Maxine. "Hey," I say. "Thanks for calling."

"No problem. Sorry I couldn't get back to you sooner. Our rehearsals went long this week. How are you doing?"

"Terrible!" I say. "The Sweetland Singers are coming to *Farmshine* after all, and Vanessa's put them onstage right before me!"

"Hmm," she says. "That *is* a surprise."

"And not a good one!"

"I understand why it might upset you. But let's talk about how you can handle it. What have you tried so far?"

"I tried to breathe and focus and visualize like you showed me. But I just kept imagining all these awful things happening."

"So what can you do to make visualizing work in a more positive way?"

"Nothing! Absolutely nothing!" My voice

cracks with panic. "I'm going to tell Vanessa to take my name off the program."

There's silence. Then finally Maxine says, "You're going to give up?"

"I think that's the best plan for me."

"Really? You're going to let Elaine Winton and the Sweetland Singers intimidate you? And all because you have a unique voice that isn't suited to a treble choir?" I can hear the frustration in Maxine's voice. "Honestly, Paisley, I thought you had more guts."

"I'm really sorry," I say. "But I just don't."

"Well, if your mind's made up, there's nothing more I can do for you. If you want to spend the rest of your life regretting that you never made anything of your talent, go right ahead. It's your decision. Just please don't waste any more of my time."

Ouch.

I know she's right. But my whole body is shaking. I try to settle myself with some deep breathing. Am I really going to let Maxine down? Am I really going to let myself down? "Okay, wait," I say. "I'll stick it out. I'm going to sing!"

"Good. That's what I wanted to hear."

"So are we still on for Saturday?" I ask.

"Yes, I will see you then. And Paisley?"

"Yes, Maxine?"

"You need to remember that show business is tough. You have to be prepared for all kinds of surprises and screwups and so on. Expect the best, but be prepared for anything. You can't let anything throw you."

"I won't," I say. "Thank you so much for your help."

"I am here for you anytime," she says. "As long as you're not quitting."

"I'm not quitting."

"Good. I have an idea. Why don't you think of it this way: the Sweetland Singers are *opening* for you."

Ooh, I like that. The Sweetland Singers are opening for me!

I hang up the phone. I feel relieved and inspired for a full ten minutes. Then our land line rings. We hardly ever get calls on it, except for telemarketers. But it's kind of late for that. I answer, just in case Mom's phone died or something and she's trying to reach me.

It's Cadence. "Hey, Pissley," she says. "Why'd you block me?"

I should hang up. But instead I ask, "What do you want?"

Cadence laughs. "Oh, just to see how you're doing with your stage fright. You must be *so* scared now that the show is only days away."

"I'm fine," I say, trying to keep my voice calm.

"Well, that's good," she says. "Because there's going to be, like, four hundred people there. And they'll all be waiting to hear the girl Maxine Gaston chose for private lessons sing!" Her jealousy sizzles down the line. "And they're going to want their money back when they hear your awful voice. Or when they don't hear you, because you probably won't even be able to choke out the words at all."

Okay, enough. "You know what, Cadence? I'm really sorry Maxine wouldn't take you on as a client," I say. "But I guess she felt I had more talent and potential." I hope I don't regret this. "I mean, Maxine would know a star when she sees one, right?"

"Oh, she'll see one at *Farmshine*, all right," she says in a threatening tone. "I'm the soloist for the

Sweetland Singers, and I'm going to blow every-body away!"

"Congratulations!" I say as sweetly as I can. "Good luck with that."

"And Heath's going to give me flowers," she says. "Because he's my boyfriend, not yours. No guy would ever like you, Pissley McFatland."

I hang up.

Twelve

On Saturday afternoon I walk over to Riverside House for my rehearsal. As usual, I sing to myself on the way, warming up my voice. I'm feeling super positive. If I want to be a star, I have to think and act like one.

Maxine has helped me a lot. When I first met her, I knew nothing. *Nothing.* Except that I wanted to be a singer but was scared to go onstage. But in just a few sessions she has taught me so much. And I really feel like I'm ready for the next step.

I'm going to sing for my best friend and her parents. And I'm going to blow them away. And then I'll be in great shape for singing in front of four hundred people at the big show.

When Jasmeer meets me at the door she says, "Cool outfit."

"You think?" I'm wearing black leggings, gray-and-red-striped work socks, a black tank with a plaid shirt overtop and a gray tweed hipster vest on top of that.

Jasmeer nods her approval. "Love the vest."

"I snuck it from my dad's closet. He's had it forever, and it's too small for him now so he never wears it. I altered it to fit me." I spent the morning with a needle and thread, trying to get it just right. Trying to stay calm.

"Hey, I didn't know you could sew."

"My mom taught me." It was something we actually enjoyed doing together, music being such a source of conflict. "Maybe I should have worn something fancier?"

"You look perfect."

"I didn't want to dress up too much, because it's only a rehearsal. Just you and your parents, right?"

"Right."

"No B&B guests?"

"None that you need to worry about," Jasmeer says. "There's a couple checked in, but they've gone to dinner and a movie. They won't be back until late."

"You're sure?"

"I'm sure. I looked up the movie listings for them. Their show doesn't even start until nine o'clock."

"I'm still nervous, though, even if I'm only singing for you and your parents."

"Well, don't be. We're your biggest fans."

"Based on never having heard me sing. Ever. But thanks for the vote of confidence."

"Maxine is waiting for you, rock star." Jasmeer gives me a gentle push toward the guest lounge. "See you later."

Maxine is at the piano, playing my song. She nods at me to come right in and start. When we've run through it, she smiles and says, "Excellent! You must have worked really hard this week."

"I did practice a lot. Everything. And I'm sorry for, you know, panicking about the Sweetland Singers. I won't let them get to me."

Maxine stands up from the piano bench. "That's the attitude."

"I hope you're not mad at me."

"Look," she says. "The only thing that will make me mad is if you give up. And since you're here, you obviously haven't, so all is well." She closes the lid on the piano.

"But shouldn't we keep working on the song?"

"You don't want to leave your best performance in rehearsal. Save it for the stage. Or in this case, for after dinner. And speaking of dinner, Sunita said it's ready anytime, so let's go eat."

Dinner smells great, but I can't imagine eating anything. My stomach is saying no, no, no. "Can't we do the singing first?" I ask. "Get it over with?"

But Maxine is already on her way to the dining room. Why didn't I realize sooner that performing after dinner was a bad idea? But I was focused on being able to sing at all. I'll have to pretend to eat, so Sunita won't notice and think I don't like the food.

At the table, all anyone wants to talk about is *Farmshine.* Jasmeer blabs on about selling her cards and prints. Her dad blabs on about his sunflower cookies. Maxine blabs on about being the MC for such a great show.

I wish they'd all shut up. Or at least discuss something else. Then Sunita asks if my mom and dad are coming to the show. She passes a basket of fresh warm rolls around. "Jasmeer's told me how busy they are."

"Yeah, they are. I mean, they're busy, but they are coming."

"I imagine they are pleased about your singing?"

Yeah, right. I take a roll. "Mmm, this smells so good." Maybe I can tear it into pieces and hide them in my pocket.

"Craig made them," Sunita says. "He needed a break from sunflower cookies." She waits, but I don't laugh. Or answer her question. Finally she says, "Well, we'd love to meet your parents. Whenever they're available."

"Okay, I'll tell them." Time to change the subject again. "Hey, anybody else excited for the Santa Claus parade next weekend? I've gone every year since we moved to Stonehill." And this year I'll enjoy it even more than usual, because the show will be over by then. "Want to go with me, Jas?"

"Sure," she says.

"I'm really hoping we can all go," Jasmeer's mom says. "Since this is our first year here, we've never been." She passes a platter of roasted vegetables. "And we've also never heard the famous Sweetland Singers, but I understand they're performing at the fundraiser too, so I'm also really looking forward to that."

Oh my god. I almost drop the platter. How did changing the subject lead straight to the Sweetland Singers?

"Help yourself," Sunita says. "There's lots more in the kitchen."

I can't possibly eat anything. "Thanks, but I'm good."

"Another wonderful dinner, Sunita," Maxine says. "Really delicious."

"Were you ever a member of the Sweetland Singers?" Jasmeer's dad asks me. "You seem like a natural for a group like that."

"Um, no. Not really my thing."

"Paisley is just as talented as anyone in the Sweetland Singers," Maxine says. "But she's more of a solo act." I flush with pride. And hope I don't throw up.

Sunita looks at my plate of food. I've hardly eaten anything. But all she says is, "Well, then, if everyone's finished, why don't we have dessert later and listen to Paisley's solo right now?"

Everyone agrees and heads to the lounge.

I rush to the bathroom first. I have to pee. And I wish I'd brought a toothbrush. Why didn't I think of that? I rinse my mouth out as best I can, putting some toothpaste from the cabinet on my finger.

I look at myself in the mirror. My hair looks so wimpy. I grab an elastic from my pocket and pull a random bunch into a wonky little ponytail on top of my head.

The bit of food I ate feels like lead in my stomach. Jasmeer knocks on the door. "You okay? We're all waiting for you."

"I'm fine. I'll be there in a minute."

"Great. Good luck!"

I do some deep breathing to calm my jitters. Then I force myself to stride out of the bathroom like a star.

This is it. This is my big test.

Thirteen

When I enter the lounge, Jasmeer and her parents are settled on the sofa. Maxine is at the piano. They're all smiling at me. I smile back, standing up tall and strong as Maxine taught me.

There's nothing to worry about. Really. I couldn't have a friendlier, more receptive audience. They want me to succeed.

And I want to entertain them. I gather my energy and focus. I can do this!

"Ready?" Maxine asks.

"Ready."

"Ladies and gentlemen," Maxine says. "I'm delighted to introduce tonight's star performer, Miss Paisley McFarland. This young lady has an astounding voice, and I just know you're going to enjoy her rendition of 'Somewhere the Music Shines Bright.'"

Jasmeer and her parents break into wild applause. "Woohoo!" Jasmeer hoots. "Go, girl!"

I gulp air. I wasn't expecting that introduction. But of course Maxine would do her full-on MC act.

Breathe, breathe, breathe.

Maxine slides into the intro. She cues me, and I come in right on time. Right on pitch. Just like I've practiced.

I can feel Jasmeer and her parents go still. They're spellbound. Because I'm better than they expected!

First verse done well. Chorus too. Keep the energy flowing. I go into the second verse.

There's a noise at the front door. Someone's coming into Riverside House! They're talking and laughing. Everyone turns to see what's going on.

The B&B guests must be back early.

Sunita leaps up and rushes to greet them.

I look to Maxine for help. She mouths the words *keep singing.*

I do my best to carry on.

But instead of ushering the guests upstairs to their rooms, Sunita brings them into the lounge and sits them in the two wing chairs by the window. They smile politely.

The breath goes out of me. This can't be happening.

Maxine stops playing. "Welcome," she says, like she was expecting them and is glad they're here. "Thank you so much for joining us. For your listening pleasure, and if it's all right with Paisley, we'll start again." I am stunned but manage a nod. She goes back to the intro.

For her sake, I have to try. She's spent so much time coaching me. I owe her.

I open my mouth, but nothing comes out.

My heart pounds, and sweat pours down my body.

Maxine keeps playing, swinging back to the intro twice, as if that was always the plan.

I try to come in again, but my throat has closed up. I couldn't make a sound right now to save my life!

I can't get a grip. I think I'm going to throw up. I panic and race out of the lounge. Right back to the bathroom off the kitchen.

But instead of being sick, I collapse on the floor and begin to sob.

In a few minutes Jasmeer knocks and comes in. "It's okay now," she says. "The guests have gone upstairs."

I can't speak. I crouch on the floor beside the toilet and sob some more.

"Hey, c'mon. You did great."

That stops my crying. "No, I didn't. I sucked big-time. And Maxine will be so mad at me. After all she did to help me, I let her down."

Jasmeer sits on the floor beside me. "She's not mad. She just wants to talk to you."

I can't stay in the bathroom forever. I need to get this over with and go home. Then I can cry all night if I want to. Which I do.

What a total disaster! How can I be a star if I can't even deal with two extra people in the audience?

I use a lot of tissue to dry the sweat from my back, neck and armpits. I hope I don't smell too bad. I need to use way more deodorant for *Farmshine*. That's if Maxine doesn't kick me off the program.

And even if Maxine is willing to give me another chance, I don't know if I can do it. I don't have what it takes. I'll never overcome my stage fright.

I use more tissue to wipe the mascara smeared around my eyes. I yank out the ridiculous little spike of a ponytail. I drink some water and do some breathing.

Why is it easy enough to breathe now? Why couldn't I take control when I needed to? Why am I so useless?

I almost start crying again, but Jasmeer gives me a hug. "Hey, hey, it's okay," she says. "That's what a rehearsal is for."

"It's not okay," I say. "And it's never going to be. I'm done."

"No, you're not." Jasmeer drags me into the kitchen. Her parents and Maxine are there. "We have to talk about what happened," she says.

All eyes are on me. Before anyone else can speak, I say, "Sorry, everyone. I blew it and I'm really, really sorry."

"No, I'm sorry," Sunita says. "I shouldn't have brought those guests in with no warning."

Jasmeer says, "Yeah, Mom. That was not cool."

"They skipped the movie because the roads were so bad, and they wanted to get back before it got worse. I just thought they'd enjoy hearing you sing, Paisley."

Jasmeer says, "But the whole idea was that it would be just us, for practice, to help Paisley get over her stage fright."

"I know, I know. I was just so amazed by how good she is! I wanted the whole world to hear her."

"Thanks, Sunita," I say. "Please don't worry about it. I'm the one who messed up. I should totally be able to handle stuff like that."

Silence.

Everyone looks at Maxine. She's leaning against the counter with her arms crossed. We're all waiting to hear what she says.

I can't meet her eye. She's going to explode now for sure. She's going to tell me to forget all about being a famous pop star.

Because when things got tough, I freaked.

I gave up and ran away.

Maxine paces once around the kitchen. Then she says, "Actually, Sunita, it's a good thing you did bring those guests in. Paisley is right. She needs to be able to deal with distractions and unexpected disasters onstage." She moves toward the kitchen doorway. "Paisley, may I speak to you?"

"I'm really sorry," I say to her out in the hall. "I tried my best, but I just lost it."

"Yes," says Maxine. "It makes me wonder. Are you serious about chasing your dream?"

I am not a bit surprised by her cold tone. But there's something I need to find out. Instead of replying, I ask, "Did you know those people were coming?"

"No, I had no idea. Why would you think that?"

"Because you were so cool about it. You acted like they were invited."

Maxine sighs. "Have I taught you nothing? A professional must always expect the unexpected. Whatever it is, make it work." She starts up the stairs, but then turns. "You never answered my question, Paisley."

I'll never forgive myself if I quit now. I stand straight and breathe like I'm about to sing. "My answer is yes," I say. "Yes, I'll do whatever it takes."

"I'm glad to hear that. Then I shall see you at the theater for soundcheck Thursday night. You know what you have to do between now and then. Better get to it."

Fourteen

Despite my declaration, I'm still not sure I can go through with it. Maybe I can pretend to be sick. If I had laryngitis, I'd have to cancel.

But Maxine would know I was faking. She would be disappointed in me.

More important, *I* would be disappointed in me.

You know what you have to do, Maxine said.

I agree. But will it be enough?

To make matters worse, Cadence keeps taunting me at school. Whenever she sees me in the hall, she calls me Pissley McFartland and holds her nose, or Pissley McFatland and makes a piggy face. But then she posts stuff on the Facebook page like *Paisley McFarland is going to shine at Farmshine!*

She's trying to rattle me. And it's working.

I can't stop her. But on Wednesday in math class, I get an idea about how to get over the trauma of the rehearsal disaster. Maybe if I make myself relive it, I can change the ending.

So after dinner that night I go to my room and visualize singing at Riverside House again. But this time I don't stop when the unexpected guests arrive. I don't let them scare me. I don't let them distract me. I carry on with my performance, and everyone loves it!

By the time Jasmeer's dad drives us to the Stonehill Theater for the soundcheck on Thursday night, I'm feeling better about things. Not over-confident, but quietly in control.

A volunteer greets us at the door and checks our names off a list. "Vanessa wants everyone seated out front in fifteen minutes."

"I'm going to have a quick look around," I say to Jasmeer. "Maxine told me to check out everything beforehand so I'll feel more comfortable onstage. Want to come with me?"

"Sure," she says. "I need shots of everything anyway and lots of candid stuff too."

We head down a hallway crowded with kids all talking and laughing with excitement. The green room and dressing rooms are crammed too, with performers tuning their instruments and dancers stretching. People are fussing with their hair and makeup or taking selfies.

It hits me that these performers all have training and experience. Some have a little, some a lot. But everyone in the show has been onstage before except me. All I've got is raw talent.

And stage fright.

At least the Sweetland Singers aren't here. They're having their regular rehearsal tonight and will do their soundcheck tomorrow, right before the show. Still, I want to get away from the other performers. So after Jasmeer has taken a few photos, I say, "I want to go check out the stage."

We head for the wings, where we watch the sound crew setting up their equipment. Thank goodness Maxine warned me it would be chaotic.

"I'm going out there," I say. Jasmeer follows, snapping photos of everything.

I gaze at the three sets of red curtains, at the stage lights, out at the sound booth and the four hundred theater seats. I realize something a bit weird. Even though I felt intimidated around the other performers backstage, I don't feel that way here. Standing at center stage, it feels like there's a special space around me. A space just waiting to be filled with my voice.

"You okay?" Jasmeer asks. "Not too overwhelmed?"

I grab a microphone off a stand to get the feel of it. "Actually, this is fine! I love it!"

"Hey, you can test that later," a stage hand snaps at me. "Right now we need you out of the way."

"Oh, sorry." Doesn't matter. I've seen enough to know I want to be singing for an audience. I'm ready to try.

"Let's go," I tell Jasmeer. We take the stage steps down into the auditorium, where the other performers and volunteers are gathering. Vanessa is beginning her announcements as we slip into seats.

"Welcome, everybody," Vanessa says. "We have a lot to do tonight, so I'd appreciate your attention and patience." She waits while the room goes quiet. "Okay! We're here to practice getting you on and offstage as quickly and efficiently as possible, and to set the lights and monitors. We don't have a lot of time, so each of you will do just the beginning and end of your acts."

There's a buzz as everyone discusses that. We all knew that's what would happen, but apparently some performers need to talk about it anyway.

"Quiet, please!" Vanessa calls. "Once you're done onstage, you're free to go. You're also welcome to stay and watch, but if you do, please be quiet and respectful." She waits again while the chattering stops. "And one more thing, people. I am pleased to announce that *Farmshine* is officially sold out!"

The cheering is so loud that Vanessa has to yell into her microphone. "So if anybody has a ticket they can't use, please let us know! There's a long waiting list too. Okay, first-half performers, backstage now! Let's do this!"

To make sure I stay hydrated, I sip from my water bottle as the different first-half acts go through their checks. There's an Elvis tribute artist, a ukulele band, the Stonehill High Jazz Band and some amazing dancers.

And through it all I'm super aware of Maxine up on the stage, doing her intros like the pro she is. She makes funny jokes in her famous actor's voice and puts everyone at ease. Such a pro.

I'm feeling a bit shy about talking to her after the other night. I hope she's not still mad at me.

"Okay, that's a wrap for the first half," Vanessa finally announces. "Let's take a quick break, everybody. There are drinks and snacks in the green room. Second-half people, let's have you backstage in ten."

Should I go looking for Maxine?

"Let's hit the green room," Jasmeer says. "I want to snap a few photos."

Maxine is there, surrounded by a swarm of kids who want to meet Silver Spinner and get her autograph. I don't join them. I avoid the food and watch Jasmeer taking her pictures. Then Vanessa is calling everyone to their places.

I hurry to the wings.

"So." Maxine's voice behind me makes me jump. "Have you checked out the venue?"

I exhale and take a deep breath. "Hi, Maxine. Yes, I made sure to have a good look around."

"Great. And are you feeling up for this?"

"Yes!"

"That is good to hear." Maxine pushes her sleeves back and pulls her reading glasses from where she's tucked them into the V neck of her sweater. She twirls them by the arm and says, "Sorry for being a bit harsh on Saturday."

"No problem. It worked."

Vanessa joins us and interrupts. "You guys all set?"

"Um, yeah," I say. "The Sweetland Singers will be on first, and then me, right?"

"They'll be up there." Vanessa points to risers arranged at the back of the stage. "When they're done, the back curtain will close in front of them, but behind the piano. Your mic is in front of that, center stage. We're already behind schedule, so we'll skip the intros, Maxine, since you know what you're doing. Okay, let's run it."

Maxine heads to the piano, and I go to the mic. She plays the intro, and I come in strong, just like we've practiced.

Except that I sound like a foghorn.

Maxine stops playing. "Hello?" she calls to the sound crew. "Way too much bass!"

I cringe. They were probably expecting me to be a soprano. We try it a few more times, until they get the settings right. When we finally skip to my last line, it sounds great.

"Awesome!" Vanessa says afterward. "Hey, Paisley, you can really sing! Who knew?"

Maxine says, "I knew."

Fifteen

At school on Friday, everyone is hyped about the show. Including me. It's a struggle to pay attention in class. I'm dazed with excitement and dread. Thrilled with what Maxine said about my singing last night at soundcheck.

Despite all the doubts that try to creep in, I keep telling myself I'm going to succeed. I was fine last night and I will be tonight. I'm going to wow the world. And maybe then my mom will actually be proud of me.

After school I dye the colored streaks in my hair darker. I apply extra deodorant and put on the outfit I've had ready for days: short denim skirt, acid-green moto jacket, multicolored infinity scarf, black leggings and lace-up black boots.

I do vocal warm-ups as I put on my stage makeup. I'm doing my lashes when our land line rings. *Nice try, Cadence. No way I'm falling for that again.*

But Mom's home early and picks up. "For you," she says, bringing the phone to my room.

"I'll call them back," I say. "I'm busy getting ready."

Mom sets the phone on my dresser. "She says it's urgent. About tonight."

I wait until Mom's out of earshot, then pick up the phone and hiss, "What do you want, Cadence?"

"Just to wish you good luck!"

"Right."

"No, really. I'm sure you're sick with nerves, and I hope your stage fright won't ruin the show."

"Anything else?"

"Actually, yes. Whatever you're wearing is seriously uncool!"

"And good luck to you too. Bye." I hang up and look at myself in the mirror. Maybe I *should* wear something else. Something funkier? Dressier? I yank clothes from my closet and drawers, but nothing feels right.

Why didn't I go shopping last week? I fling skirts and tights and jeans and tops onto my bed. Panic rises in my chest. My throat tightens.

Hang on a second, I tell myself. Do not let Cadence ruin things. Breathe. Just breathe and get a grip.

I always planned to wear this outfit onstage. Maybe it's not supercool, but it's okay. And Maxine said to wear something comfortable. Something I feel good in. So that's what I'm going to do. I ignore the heap of discarded clothes on my bed and head downstairs.

When I enter the kitchen, Mom says, "Oh, my goodness! I thought you were getting changed."

"I did."

"You're not going onstage in that?"

I don't bother to answer.

"Sorry, I mean, maybe I could lend you something?"

Way to help with my performance anxiety, Mom.

When Dad sees me, he says, "Hey, you look great!"

Mom shakes her head and asks if I want something to eat, but my stomach heaves at the thought of food. "I'll eat at the after-party," I say. "Let's just get going. I want to have lots of time for more warm-ups."

In the car, Dad wishes me luck. Mom says, "I hope Maxine Gaston helped with your nerves."

What? She hasn't checked since I told her, and she wants to know now? Right before the show? "I'm fine Mom, thanks for asking."

I wish I'd accepted the ride Jasmeer offered.

At the backstage entrance, the atmosphere is even more charged than it was last night. It's too much for me, so I make my way upstairs to the Limestone Room, where the second-half performers are supposed to wait.

But as I'm coming down the hall, I spot the Sweetland Singers in there warming up. I turn and head straight back downstairs again. No way do I need to hear them. No way do I need to see Cadence.

My phone buzzes with a text from Maxine. **Break a leg! Remember: SS opening 4 u!!!**

I text back. **Thanks!!!**

I turn my phone off and hide in a washroom stall, deep breathing until the show starts. Then

I creep out into the lobby, where volunteers are setting up for the Farmer's Market at intermission. I try to help arrange Jasmeer's cards and prints and her dad's cookies, but every move I make is wrong. I'm clumsy and in the way.

I sit on a bench and pick up a program. Jasmeer did a great job on the layout and design, using one of her sunflower photos on the cover. I flip it open, and there's my name, right after the Sweetland Singers.

There's no escaping them! Beads of sweat form on my forehead. I fan myself with the program and watch the show on a monitor.

What a difference from soundcheck. Now the stage is decorated with hay bales and paper sunflowers. Maxine looks elegant in a black silk evening suit, and the performers' costumes are stunning. Jasmeer's down in front, snapping photos like a pro.

I can't concentrate on the acts. My stomach feels full of squid tentacles. Thank heavens I didn't eat dinner. I pace the lobby on shaky legs, humming to myself to keep my voice warmed up.

Focus, focus, focus.

I run through some lines from my song. *Somewhere the music shines bright, somewhere it sounds like the sun.*

Intermission at last. I run out of the lobby before the audience crowds in. I can't risk seeing Cadence or my parents. I need a quiet space where I can pull myself together.

The backstage washroom is full, so I find a deserted corner at the end of the hall. I close my eyes and breathe. I remind myself that I'm well prepared for this performance. I've followed all of Maxine's advice: I'm wearing something comfortable. I know my notes and lyrics cold. I'm familiar with the mic and the stage.

I go through my positive visualization one more time. I picture everything going well. I'm expecting the best, but I can handle anything. I am going to rock!

And then it's time. Vanessa's voice comes over the intercom. "Five minutes!"

It's showtime.

Sixteen

I rush to the wings, only to ram right into a line of thirty or so kids wearing black pants and white shirts. The Sweetland Singers. Again! I stop short and stay well behind them, ignoring Cadence. I don't take my place in the wings until they've paraded onto the risers.

I can see Ms. Winton in the dim light, making sure everyone stands exactly where she wants them. I hear Maxine introduce them. And then the curtain opens and the lights go up to enthusiastic applause.

Ms. Winton sweeps onstage and takes a quick bow, then turns and leads the choir in their first number.

It's a ballad about a river, and it starts with a soprano solo. The solo Cadence bragged about.

Her voice rings bright and clear. When the choir joins in, the sound is rich and effortless, almost like flowing water. The effect is spellbinding, and the audience loves it.

"Thank you very much," Ms. Winton says. "That was 'Song of the River,' and as many of you know, it's our signature song, since we're named for Stonehill's Sweetland River." She pauses dramatically, looking elegant in her long black dress, her sleek silver hair swept up into a French twist. "And I must say that we're absolutely delighted to be here tonight to share our music with you and help raise funds to save Sunflower Farm."

Just hearing Ms. Winton's plumy voice gives me a flashback to that horrible audition. *Could you try it again, an octave higher?* And then, *I'm sorry dear...but I can't offer you a place...*

Breathe, breathe, breathe, I tell myself. Stay in control.

I stare at the stage backdrop the volunteers painted, a field of sunflowers against a blue sky. So pretty. I study the singers. I find it odd that they're standing with their hands behind their backs, but they do look very confident and professional.

Well, I won't be intimidated. As Maxine put it, the Sweetland Singers are opening for me.

"Our next number we learned especially for tonight," Ms. Winton says. "It's a country song from the 1970s called 'Sunflower,' and it's such fun. We hope you'll enjoy it as much as we do. Our soloist, as in our river song, is the lovely Cadence Wang."

"Sunflower" is an upbeat, feel-good song. Halfway through it, the singers swing their hands up in front of them, showing off the paper sunflowers they've been hiding. They move side to side in unison, making their sunflowers wave and sway. It looks like they're all part of the sunflower-field background.

The audience cheers like crazy and claps along.

When the song is over, Ms. Winton and the Sweetland Singers take a bow. The curtain closes, and they march off the risers. The audience is calling, "More! More!"

The breath has gone out of me. The Sweetland Singers were fantastic! No wonder they've won so many awards.

Maxine was wrong. They didn't open for me. They stole the show!

I swallow hard, trying not to cry. What was I thinking, dyeing my hair and wearing this stupid outfit? I should have worn something simple and black, like Maxine and Ms. Winton. Like Mom wanted to lend me.

Why did I ever sign up to sing?

I can't do this. I have to get out of here.

But Maxine is already back at the podium. "Ladies and gentlemen," she says. "How about those Sweetland Singers? Their name says it all, doesn't it?" She waits through renewed applause. "A huge thank-you to them for making the time to be here." She waits again for quiet. "And now it is my very great pleasure to introduce our next performer. Paisley McFarland, a ninth-grade student here at Stonehill High, is making her debut tonight. And while this might be her first public performance, I know for sure it won't be her last! You're in for a real treat!"

More applause. They're clapping for *me.* I can hear Jasmeer chanting, "Paisley, Paisley, Paisley!" Just like I visualized.

Maxine believes in me. I can't let her down. No. I can't let *myself* down.

The only way to overcome my stage fright is to do exactly what Maxine taught me.

Focus, focus, focus.

I rush onstage with a big smile, arms raised in acknowledgment, waving to the audience. Maybe my voice won't work, but I'm going to sell my entrance. I look left, right, then up into the balcony. The spotlight is blinding. I look down at the front rows.

I can't pick out faces in the darkness, but I know where my parents are sitting. They're out there, along with most of Stonehill. And I'm going to show them I'm a star.

I take my place at the mic as Maxine takes hers at the piano.

She plays the intro, and I'm in:

Dark universe
No more music, no more songs
Silent days and nights
All our melodies are gone.

On time. On pitch. Perfect!

I channel my fear into the emotion of the song, wooing the audience and drawing them in.

Who can ever find them?
Who can bring back harmony?
We have to find a way
to the Lost Song Galaxy.

I have their full attention, and I hold them close. Adrenaline surges through me, creating a power and joy beyond anything I've ever experienced.

And then the back door of the theater opens.

There's a shift of energy in the audience.

Folks start to whisper, and heads turn.

I'm losing them.

What's going on?

Who cares? I'm not stopping. Whatever is happening out there, I'm not going to let it distract me. I'm not messing up again like I did at Riverside House.

I sing the final chorus, building in volume.

Somewhere the music shines bright
Somewhere it sounds like the sun
Somewhere in darkness our songs still live on
Oh, somewhere the music shines bright!

I am on fire! I hold the last note longer than I've ever been able to before. I even have enough air left to pronounce the final *t*.

Maxine stops playing, and there's polite applause. But most people are up and out of their seats. They're gawking at the person who just slipped in and is standing at the back. Phones and cameras are flashing, even though flash photography is prohibited.

When the lights come up, I see why.

Oh my god!

It's *Denzi*!

She's wearing a ballcap and sunglasses, her hair in a ponytail, but it's definitely her.

Oh my god!

Still, even Denzi is not going to distract me.

I stay in star mode, take a deep bow and strut offstage.

Nobody even notices.

Seventeen

I pause in the wings. What just happened?

I can hear Maxine trying to take control of the situation. "That was a fabulous performance!" she announces. "Let's hear it for Paisley McFarland!"

But it's no use. They're all swarming Denzi.

"Folks!" Maxine commands in her booming voice. "Please take your seats! Now! The show must go on!"

A few people obey, probably those who already got pictures.

"Thank you," Maxine says. "Yes, it appears that a surprise celebrity has entered the building. And I'm going to call her up onstage later. But first let's give our full attention to the terrific lineup of performers ready and waiting to entertain you."

Gradually the rest of the people settle back into their seats.

I head to the Limestone Room, where the volunteers are getting ready for the after-party. Some are setting up tables. Some are bringing in platters of sandwiches and wraps. Others are organizing the nonalcoholic bar with soda, water and fruit punch. I had been looking forward to celebrating after the show, but not anymore.

I don't even try to help. I collapse on a bench and stare at a monitor. Next up is a metal band whose drummer went to Stonehill High, then an *a cappella* quartet and then more dancers.

I watch in a daze. Did Maxine know Denzi was coming?

Oh my god. How awesome would it be if I got to meet her?

Mainly, though, I'm just relieved my performance is over.

I should be thrilled. I did great out there. I didn't panic, and I handled the interruption to end all interruptions. But if I'm honest, I have to admit that I feel a bit deflated. Okay, totally devastated.

I wanted major applause. I wanted *glory*!

But hey, Denzi is here. She's actually here! How can I blame the audience for being distracted? If I'd been sitting out there, I would have done the exact same thing.

The volunteers finish their setup jobs and come crowding around the monitor to watch Maxine close the show. I wait for them to compliment me on my singing. Or at least mention how great it was that I carried on when Denzi interrupted my performance. Nothing.

And then I realize they wouldn't have even seen the end of my performance. The cameras would all have been on Denzi.

Now the cameras are all on Maxine. She sits at the piano and sings her Silver Spinner song, "The Universe Is Made of Music."

"She's *incredible*," one volunteer says.

"Totally," another says.

"I can't believe Denzi's here too," another says. "Hey, Paisley, were you surprised that she showed up in the middle of your song? Do you think she's going to sing?"

Everyone turns to stare. I keep my eyes on the monitor. "I didn't know she was coming, and I have no idea what's going on."

When Maxine is done, the audience chants, "Encore! Encore!"

She finishes with a flourish, stands and takes a deep bow, then strolls back to the podium. "Thank you so much," she says. "You've been a great audience. And now, as promised, our celebrity guest." She points to the back of the auditorium. "Come on up here, Denzi."

The audience goes beyond wild, screaming, clapping, cheering.

Denzi yanks off her ballcap and sunglasses, tossing them into the crowd. She prances up the aisle and onto the stage, waving and blowing kisses to her fans. She embraces Maxine, then takes her mic and calls, "Hello, Stonehill! How y'all doing? It's nice to be back!"

Mad, crazy cheering.

"Thank y'all so much. You're too kind." Denzi smiles and waves some more. Even in ripped jeans, cowboy boots and a sunflower-yellow T-shirt, she's gorgeous. And she's so at ease. She owns the stage.

"Okay then, folks, listen up. When my friend Maxine from *The Lost Song Galaxy* movie called me about this fundraiser, I knew I had to be here.

I'm so happy I made it!" Hoots and whistles from the crowd. Finally it's quiet enough for her to speak again. "Stonehill is my hometown, and Sunflower Farm is a very special place to me. And so it gives me great pleasure to announce that I'm making a donation of fifty thousand dollars to the Save Sunflower Farm fund." She has to stop while the audience goes even wilder.

That's a huge donation! Imagine having that much money! And how cool for Heath and Vanessa and their mom!

Denzi is speaking again. "One more thing. My timing is terrible. When I arrived, I accidentally interrupted a young lady's performance. That was rude of me, and I sincerely apologize. I should have stayed out in the lobby, but when I saw her on the monitor I just had to come in and hear her in person. And now I hope she'll let me make it up to her. Paisley, where are you? Can you please come back up here?"

I gasp. Did Denzi just call *me* up onstage?

I'm so shocked, I can't move.

One of the volunteers pushes me to stand. "Go on!" she urges. "What are you waiting for? Get up there!"

I scurry back into the auditorium, up the main aisle and onto the stage. I stand there staring out at the audience, stunned. Is this really happening? Is it possible? Somehow my eyes land right on my parents. The look on Mom's face is priceless.

"Hi, Paisley!" Denzi says, giving me a hug.

I try to reply, but no words come out.

"I love how you were singing my song," she says quickly, filling the dead air. "Wanna do it again, together?"

There's no time to react. No time to panic. Maxine is already at the piano playing the intro. Like they planned it.

And then I'm singing. Singing with Denzi. Standing so close I can count the beaded silver bracelets stacked on her arms from wrist to elbow. Standing so close I can smell her spicy perfume and see her sunflower earrings.

Jasmeer steps up close to us, snapping photos. Vanessa is there too, shooting video. Throughout the theater flashes go off like fireworks.

I try to blend my voice with Denzi's. It feels easy and right, like we've tapped into some universal vibration. Denzi is harmonizing on higher notes while I take the lower, and it sounds like we've been rehearsing for weeks!

Denzi starts dancing, and I follow with ease. Nothing fancy, just totally free. When we're done, Denzi grabs my hand and we bow together. The thunderous applause goes on and on and on.

Take that, Sweetland Singers.

Eighteen

After the final curtain call with all the performers crowded onstage, Denzi takes my arm and leads me down the steps into the audience. Fans fall in beside and behind us, gushing words like "fabulous" and "fantastic!" I'm not sure if they mean Denzi or me or us singing together. But who really cares?

"Oh my god, thank you so, so much," I babble to Denzi. "That was awesome, the best thing I've ever done, and I love your music and—"

"You bet." Denzi cuts me off before I make a complete fool of myself. "Maxine was right. You've got raw talent. You could have a great career ahead of you."

"Seriously? You really think so?"

"You've got the voice and the stage presence. Lots of potential."

"Thanks!"

"But it takes more than that. It takes a whole lot of dedication. You need to be prepared to work hard." *Oh, I am. Believe me.*

We reach the lobby, and the crowd following behind forms a circle around us. Denzi accepts a pen from a fan and then she's busy signing programs and posing for pictures. It's like I'm not even there.

I search the lobby for Maxine. She's swarmed too, but I push to the front of the line. "Excuse me," I say as I grab her arm and pull her off to the side. "I just need to talk to Maxine for one minute."

"Hey, congratulations," Maxine says. "You were wonderful."

"Thanks, but I have to ask. You told Denzi about *Farmshine*?"

"Yes, as I said onstage. Why do you ask?"

"But did you know she was coming?" It's hard to keep a quiver of anger out of my voice. Because if Maxine knew and didn't tell me...

"No, Paisley. Just like when those guests came back early to Riverside House, I didn't know. Denzi told me she couldn't make it. I was just as surprised as everybody else when she showed up."

Should I believe her? And does it even matter?

"Honestly," she says. "I wouldn't do that to you."

"But you might have thought I'd be too scared to go on if I knew."

"If I knew, I would have told you and we would have talked about it, so you could be prepared."

"Okay. Sorry."

"The most important thing to remember is that you dealt with it. You were prepared and professional."

Yes, I was. I really was. "Yeah, you're right. Thank you, Maxine. For everything."

"My pleasure, Paisley. I look forward to watching your career unfold."

Maxine looks across the lobby at Denzi, who is trying to escape from her fans to her waiting limo. She makes a "call me" sign at Maxine before her fans chase her right out the door, cameras and phones flashing.

A volunteer who's been standing back, waiting patiently for us to finish talking, reaches her phone forward and says, "Can I please get a selfie with you, Silver Spinner?"

I leave Maxine to her fans and go find Jasmeer.

"Yay!" she says. "You were amazing! I had goose bumps."

"Thanks. I can't believe I sang with Denzi!"

"Too cool," Jasmeer says. "And we sold out of cards and cookies. Oops, heads up. Here come your parents."

I turn to see Mom and Dad pushing through the crowd. "Hi!" says Jasmeer. "Wasn't she just awesome?"

"Yup," Dad says, hugging me. "She rocked." He hands me a mixed bouquet wrapped in paper printed with sunflowers. "These are for you, superstar."

"Thanks, Dad."

My eyes meet Mom's. "Congratulations," she says as she comes in for a hug too. "Excellent performance. And I didn't think I'd ever say this, but maybe pop is right for you."

What? I'm speechless. But I hug her back.

"If you were nervous, it didn't show," she says. "And you were really brave to keep singing after that woman barged in."

Have aliens abducted my mother? "Thanks!" My voice trembles with emotion. "That means a lot to me."

Mom scans the lobby. "Now where is that MC? I want to meet her and thank her for helping you."

"You mean Maxine? She's around here somewhere."

"Well, maybe I'll catch her later. Look, there's Elaine Winton," Mom says. "Over here!" she calls across the noisy crowd.

Ms. Winton glides toward our group. "Well done," she says to me. "Very impressive."

My mouth drops open. "Um, thanks. And I really liked your singers. Especially when they did the sunflower song."

"Oh, they were just angelic," Mom says. "That sunflower number was magical. And your soloist was fantastic! It's too bad Paisley turned down the chance to sing with you."

Ms. Winton looks from me to Mom and back, eyebrows raised. "Well, yes," she finally says.

"But it seems that Paisley made the best choice for her unique talent."

I give her a nod of thanks. Maybe she's not such a dragon after all.

"You know, I really think she did," Mom says. "What a voice! And even if pop's not my kind of thing, I'm so glad Paisley has music in her blood."

And then Cadence rushes up with Heath. "Hey, Paisley," she says. *So I'm not Pissley anymore?* "Coaching with Maxine *and* singing with Denzi?" She sniffs and wipes at her eyes. *Is she trying not to cry?* "How did you manage that?"

I smile and say, "Congratulations to you too, Cadence. Your solo was awesome."

She ignores my compliment. "Are you planning to audition for the school musical?"

So *that's* what she's worried about. "You bet I am."

"But there probably won't be a part for a girl with such a low voice. I mean, they'll probably want a soprano like me."

She might be right. But maybe not. "We'll see," I say. "Nice flowers, by the way." She's holding a bouquet just like mine. Volunteers were selling them in the lobby at intermission.

"Oh, these are from Heath." She pulls him closer to her. "He's such a great boyfriend."

I try to catch his eye, but no luck. Okay. Whatever. Because I sang with Denzi! And she said I have a chance at a musical career!

By the time Jasmeer and I get to the after-party in the Limestone Room, the food is mostly gone. A lot of people try to talk to me, but I'm done. I just want to go home.

*　*　*

Jasmeer calls early the next day. I'm barely awake. "Have you seen it?" she asks.

I'm still groggy and don't know what she means. "Huh? Seen what?"

"Get on YouTube right now!"

I boot up my tablet. "What am I looking for?"

"Vanessa's *Farmshine* video. It's gone viral."

I find it and see Denzi singing onstage with me. "Whoa."

"Yeah, pretty amazing," Jasmeer says. "And apparently we made a ton of money, even before Denzi's donation."

I wasn't really listening to her. "I sound great," I say. "Really great."

"Of course you do," Jasmeer says. "And if you come over this afternoon, we can go through the photos I took last night. I got some cool ones of you."

"Okay, later." I hang up so I can watch the video again. I know it's just because of Denzi that it's getting so many views. But still, it makes me want to finally post one of my own.

Time to get going on that whole lot of work and dedication Denzi mentioned.

If I can sing onstage, I can do anything.